For Justin Chanda, who helped me find my books

SIMON & SCHUSTER BOOKS FOR YOUNG READERS
An imprint of Simon & Schuster Children's Publishing Division
1230 Avenue of the Americas, New York, New York 10020
Copyright © 2015 by Debbie Ridpath Ohi
SIMON & SCHUSTER BOOKS FOR YOUNG READERS is a trademark of Simon & Schuster, Inc.
For information about special discounts for bulk purchases, please contact Simon & Schuster Special Sales at 1-866-506-1949
or business@simonandschuster.com.
The Simon & Schuster Speakers Bureau can bring authors to your live event. For more information or to book an event,
contact the Simon & Schuster Speakers Bureau at 1-866-248-3049 or visit our website at www.simonspeakers.com.
Book design by Laurent Linn
The text for this book is set in ITC Highlander Std.
The illustrations for this book are rendered digitally.
Manufactured in China
0215 SCP
2 4 6 8 10 9 7 5 3 1
Library of Congress Cataloging-in-Publication Data
Ohi, Debbie Ridpath, 1962- author, illustrator.
Where are my books? / Debbie Ridpath Ohi. — 1st edition.
pages cm
Summary: Spencer loves books and reads one every night, sometimes aloud, then puts the book back in its place,
but one morning his favorite book is missing, and the next day another, each replaced by a different object.
ISBN 978-1-4424-6741-5 (hardcover : alk. paper) — ISBN 978-1-4424-6742-2 (ebook)
[1. Books and reading—Fiction. 2. Lost and found possessions—Fiction. 3. Squirrels—Fiction.] I. Title.
PZ7.O414034Whe 2015
[E]—dc23
2014015990

WHERE ARE MY BOOKS?

Debbie Ridpath Ohi

SIMON & SCHUSTER BOOKS FOR YOUNG READERS

NEW YORK LONDON TORONTO SYDNEY NEW DELHI

Spencer **loved** books.

His favorite bedtime book was *Night-Night, Narwhal*.

Sometimes he read it aloud.

Every night, Spencer put the book back where it belonged.

That way he'd always be able to find it.

Until one morning . . .

"WHERE IS MY BOOK?"

Spencer looked everywhere,
but it was no use.

Night-Night, Narwhal was GONE.

That evening, he chose *Tenacious Todd*.
It was okay.

But Todd was a toad, and toads were amphibians, and amphibian
books were supposed to be for right-after-lunch story time.

When Spencer woke the next morning, *Tenacious Todd* was gone.

Every morning, another book was missing.

Next to go was *Send in the Clown Fish.*

Then *Beluga Beluga!* vanished.

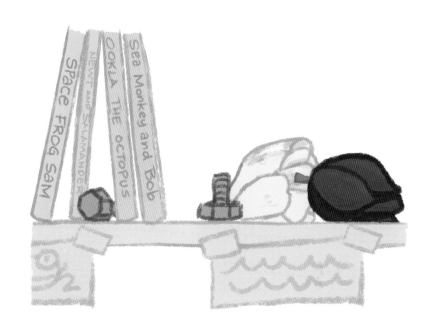

Sea Monkey and Bob went missing.

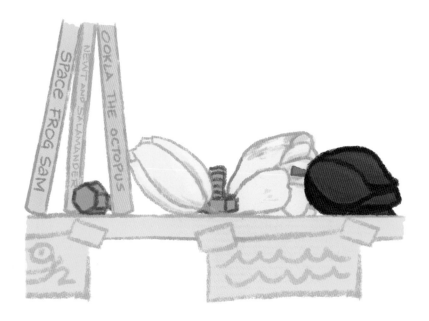

Things were getting out of hand.

Spencer vowed to find out what was going on.

His father did not know what happened
to *Night-Night, Narwhal.*

Spencer's mother had no idea either.

Nor had she seen *Tenacious Todd, Send in the Clown Fish,*
Beluga Beluga!, or any of Spencer's other missing books.

That left only ONE PERSON . . .

It was time for a new plan.

That night, Spencer set a trap with his copy of *Space Frog Sam*.

The next morning . . .

it was time for Spencer to get his books back!

Spencer ran faster.
The thief was **just around the corner.**

"AHA!" he said. "That's my . . .

"book?"

Spencer didn't know squirrels like to read.

It gave him a great idea.

Spencer told the squirrels they could borrow his books.

But there would be rules.

Just like at the library, they had to return the books they borrowed before they could borrow more.

But they didn't need to leave anything behind.

Spencer even helped them
pick out their first book.

He chose one for himself, too.

And he promised to read it aloud.